MW00877984

THE SEARCH FOR THE MISSING BANDANA

RACHAEL PETERS
ILLUSTRATIONS BY SARAH VEGA

Abbi's American Adventures
The Search for the Missing Bandana

Illustrations by Sarah Vega

Published by Lucid Books in Houston, TX.
www.LucidBooks.net

eISBN 10:1632961016
eISBN 13: 9781632961013
ISBN 10: 1632961008
ISBN 13: 9781632961006

Special Sales: Most Lucid Books titles are available in special quantity discounts. Custom imprinting or excerpting can also be done to fit special needs. Contact Lucid Books at info@lucidbooks.net.

To my incredible parents, Abbi's Granny and Poppa, thank you for sparking my love of reading, raising me to follow my dreams, encouraging me to always seek adventure, and for your unwavering support and love.

To my "sister compass"—Kelly, Ileana, Pam, and Ruth—thank you for your guidance, your direction, and most importantly, your dear friendship.

Kerplunk! Abbi dropped the mail on the floor, wagging her tail. She pulled out an envelope and ran to Rachael.

“Mom! I got a letter! It looks official.”

“Who is it from?” asked Rachael.

“Mayor Stewart! I hope I’m not in trouble. I promised I would stop barking at the cat across the street.”

“And have you been barking at the cat?”

“Only a little!”

“Well, let’s read it and see what the mayor says.”

Dear Abbi,

My granddaughter Chloe is in Miss Paling's fourth grade class. She tells me that you love to tell her class about your adventures all across America. I heard you've visited more than thirty historic cities and national parks and that you always send them postcards from your travels. Because of your great love for our nation, I would like to invite you to be the grand marshal of our annual hometown parade in three weeks. You will lead the parade on a float decorated to showcase your American adventures.

Please contact my office promptly to accept this position.

Sincerely,
Mayor Stewart

P.S.
Be sure to wear your signature patriotic bandana.

Abbi jumped up and down.

"Mom, Mom, Mom, I get to be in a parade! I've got so much to do. Invite Granny and Poppa, tell my friends, decorate a float, practice my wave, wash my bandana...Wait, where is my bandana, Mom?"

"I'm not sure, Abs. Didn't you wear it on our last big adventure?"

"I think so," barked Abbi. "I wear it on every adventure!"

"Then surely you put it away when we got home."

"Surely!" said Abbi, and she rushed off to search in her toy box, under her bed, and in the dirty clothes hamper. She even looked inside Reagan the Jeep, who drives them on all of their trips across America. Reagan is named in memory of President Ronald Reagan.

Ears drooping, Abbi returned to Rachael.

"I can't find it anywhere. I must have lost it on one of our last trips. What am I going to do, Mom? Mayor Stewart said I have to wear my patriotic bandana in the parade."

"What if you wore another one?" suggested Rachael.

"I really want to wear this one. Granny made it for me. It's one-of-a-kind! Like the mayor said, it's my signature. I always wear it to Miss Paling's class. I've worn it all over the country!"

"True, that bandana has been with us from coast to coast, from The Big Apple to the Grand Canyon and every stop in between. You're right. We've got to find it."

Abbi walked around in a circle to do some thinking. "Let's jump in the Jeep and drive to all the places we've visited! I must have lost the bandana somewhere we stopped!"

"I'm always up for an adventure, but it would take a lot of time and resources to go back to every place we've traveled," said her mom. "Plus, I have to work."

Abbi laid her head in her mom's lap and looked up at her with her big, brown eyes.

"Well, maybe I can work from the road."

Abbi nudged her mom's shoulder.

"Okay! Okay! I will arrange to work from the road. Go pack your bags for an adventure!"

"Woohoo!" howled Abbi, leaping into the air.

Abbi and Rachael began planning their trip to find the missing bandana.

"The parade is in three weeks. We've been to so many places, going back to all of them will take too long! What are we going to do?" asked Abbi.

"Hmm...what do you do when you can't solve a problem on your own?" asked Rachael.

Abbi thought and thought.

Suddenly, she yelped, "I know! What if we asked some friends to help us? When you can't solve a problem on your own, you can count on your friends to help."

Together they made a list of places the bandana might be found and a list of friends to join the search.

“Okay, so we’re going to revisit the Tyler Rose Gardens, New Orleans, Great Smoky Mountains National Park, Washington, D.C., Philadelphia, Mount Rushmore, Denver, and the Grand Canyon!” said Rachael. “What a trip this will be!”

“Yes! And we’ll call my friends all across the country and ask them to look for the bandana in the places we don’t have time to visit,” said Abbi.

GATEWAY ARCH
COLORADO ROCKIES STADIUM
NIAGARA FALLS
BOSTON FREEDOM TRAIL
STATUE OF LIBERTY
SAN DIEGO
BIG BEND
CAPULIN VOLCANO
ALAMO
VICKSBURG MILITARY PARK
FLORIDA BEACHES

Abbi was so excited that she woke up before the alarm clock the next morning. She pounced on her mom's bed and licked her face.

"Rise and shine! I packed our map, our traveling trail mix, and extra rawhides. Our road trip playlist is full of good music, and I even got your coffee ready! Let's get this adventure started!"

Abbi and Rachael loaded up their bags. Reagan the Jeep was ready to go! First stop: Tyler, Texas, the Rose Capital of the World and home of Abbi's Granny and Poppa.

Abbi jumped out of the Jeep when they arrived at the Tyler Rose Gardens.

"Let's check the gazebo where we picnicked with Granny and Poppa!" she barked.

She searched the gazebo, the pond, and the visitor center. She even made time to stop and smell the roses that filled the garden.

"Not here!" Abbi said.

"That's okay," said Rachael. "Next stop, New Orleans!"

On their first exploration of their neighbor state, they had learned that Louisiana is rich in culture, music, and wildlife. Abbi secretly hoped to see an alligator.

They searched the French Quarter in downtown New Orleans, along the cobblestone streets filled with tourists, street merchants, and horse-drawn carriages. Abbi, herding dog that she is, struggled to resist barking at the horses to keep them in line.

The sweet sound of jazz and the sugary scent of beignets filled the air, but there was no bandana to be found. “Well, Abbi, the search continues. Let’s rest here and drive to Tennessee tomorrow. Don’t forget to sign the postcard for Miss Paling’s class so we can mail it in the morning,” said Rachael.

The next day, they listened to country music on their long drive to Tennessee, a state known for great country music.

Towering trees lined the roadway along the entrance to the Great Smoky Mountains National Park. Mountains peeked through clouds that resembled billows of smoke. Reagan slowed to a stop.

“Oh wow! We’re already here!” woofed Abbi.

They retraced their steps around the park, searching for the bandana along the trail.

“Look—a park ranger!” Abbi ran over and introduced herself.

“Nice to meet you, Abbi. I’m Ranger Dan,” said the man.

“Ranger Dan, have you seen my bandana? It has stars and stripes on it! You don’t think a bear or beaver took it, do you? I’ve got to have it to lead my hometown parade,” barked Abbi.

“I haven’t seen any bears or beavers wearing a bandana, and it isn’t in the lost and found,” Ranger Dan replied. “I have friends at parks and historic sites all over the U.S. What if I ask them to look for your bandana?”

Abbi barked for joy. “That would be so helpful! Thank you, Ranger Dan. Mom and I will head to Washington, D.C., to look there!”

“Good luck, Abbi! Enjoy your visit to our nation’s capital!”

DAN

"Where should we look first? The White House?" asked Abbi when they arrived in D.C.

"Let's start with the Lincoln Memorial since last time that was your favorite. Remember the cherry blossoms we saw in the spring? What a beautiful gift to America from the country of Japan," said Rachael.

They searched the Washington Monument, which stands over 555 feet tall, encircled by American flags waving proudly in the wind.

Abbi and her mom stopped to take a photo. As Rachael readied the camera, she looked through the lens and saw Abbi chasing after a man in a military uniform.

"Abbi, stop! Come back!" shouted Rachael. She sprinted after Abbi, who was now in a full gallop chasing the man who didn't seem to notice he was being pursued.

Abbi caught up to the man and jumped on him, pawing and tugging at his pocket.

"Whoa, whoa! May I help you, pup?" asked the man in uniform.

"You've got my bandana in your pocket, sir!" she barked. Peeking out of his pocket was a red, white, and blue bandana.

"Oh, this old thing? I'm sorry, but I've had this since I joined the Marines. It's older than you are," he said.

Rachael finally reached them. "Abbi, what on earth are you doing? Why did you chase this gentleman and jump on him?"

"Hi," said the man. "I'm Major General Smith." He shook Abbi's paw and Rachael's hand.

Embarrassed, Abbi looked down. “I thought I saw my bandana in his pocket but it wasn’t mine. I’m sorry, Major General.”

The officer gave Abbi a pat on the head and wished her well on her search.

Abbi and her mom searched the Capitol, around the White House, and at the Jefferson Memorial, where Abbi selected a postcard for her pen pals. But they didn’t find the bandana.

That night, they took a stroll along the beautiful Potomac River.

“We’re never going to find my bandana, and then I won’t get to be the grand marshal of the parade,” huffed Abbi.

“I’m sure Mayor Stewart will let you marshal the parade in a different bandana,” said Rachael.

“Maybe. But it won’t be as special.”

“We have lots of friends looking for it all across the country. Either we’ll find it soon, or they will.”

Abbi woke up the next morning excited to travel to Philadelphia, Pennsylvania, the City of Brotherly Love.

“Let’s start by searching Independence Hall. Do you remember which famous documents were signed there?” asked Rachael.

"Of course, Mom. The Declaration of Independence and the Constitution. Philadelphia is the birthplace of America. Famous Americans such as Benjamin Franklin, Betsy Ross, and George Washington lived here. Our Founding Fathers walked these streets!"

Next, they investigated the Liberty Bell. Abbi felt a tap on her shoulder.

“Excuse me, my name is Ranger Carroll. Is your name Abbi?”

“Woof! Yes, my name is Abbi. How did you know that?”

“Ranger Dan is a friend of mine, and he said you and your mom would be visiting us. I’ve had the other park rangers search the area, and I hate to report your bandana isn’t here. I’m sorry.”

“Oh, man,” barked Abbi. “Thank you for your help.”

“What else will you do on your visit to Philadelphia?” asked Ranger Carroll.

Abbi and Rachael both shouted, “Get a Philly cheese steak!”

The next morning, they mailed postcards, did some souvenir shopping, and Abbi called her friends. Prissy hadn't found the bandana at the Alamo. Sophie and Josie didn't find it at Niagara Falls. Penny and Noah had come up empty at the Gateway Arch, and Ozzy didn't find it in Boston.

Everyone had enjoyed the hunt but the bandana was still missing, so off they went to South Dakota. The drive through miles and miles of radiant fields of golden sunflowers filled Abbi with hope.

"Surely, today we'll find it," she thought.

"Mount Rushmore—45 miles ahead! Almost there," said Abbi's mom. They drove up and down the narrow, windy road through Black Hills National Forest, surrounded by splendid Black Hills spruce and ponderosa pine trees.

Reagan parked by the visitor center and Abbi and Rachael walked in.

"Hi, I'm Abbi, have you seen my bandana? It's very special, my Granny made it for me and it's one-of-a-kind," barked Abbi.

"Hello there, Abbi. My name is Ruth and I am one of the park volunteers. It's nice to meet you. We heard you might be stopping by on your quest."

"Wow, you've heard about me?" barked Abbi.

"We sure have! In fact, we had some volunteers search the grounds for your bandana and I have a surprise for you," replied Ruth.

She offered Abbi a small, wrapped package.

“You found my bandana?!” Abbi cried. She tossed the package in the air and tore it open. Inside was a bandana with the faces of four presidents on it.

Abbi's head hung low. Her tail stopped wagging and drooped.

"Oh, no!" said Ruth. "Is this not a good surprise? We couldn't find your bandana, so we got you a new one with the faces carved into the Mount Rushmore monument."

"Thank you," said Abbi. "I just thought it was going to be my bandana."

"Well dear, I am sure it will turn up," said Ruth.

Abbi thanked Ruth with a big lick on the cheek and a high-five.

"I'm sorry you're disappointed, Abbi," said Mom. "It was nice for Volunteer Ruth to give you a beautiful new bandana. It looks like we get to enjoy a few more stops before we go home. Hey, tonight we can check in with more friends to see what they've found."

They hiked over to the monument, with Abbi wearing her new bandana.

Together, they enjoyed the sunset and the nightly lighting of the monument.

Four of America's greatest presidents—Washington, Jefferson, Theodore Roosevelt, and Lincoln—illuminated the night sky.

CALIFOR

After dinner and a bath at the hotel, Abbi called her friends Einstein, Daisy, Kaleb, and Jacques.

“Did you find my bandana?” she asked.

“No, sorry, Abbi,” they all said.

Abbi was disappointed but pleased to hear that they all seemed to have had a great adventure of their own. Einstein had a hot dog in Central Park and enjoyed a ferry ride to the Statue of Liberty. Maybe Pretzel, Addie, or Kutta would have good news tomorrow.

“Up and at ‘em, Abbi! Today we start the long drive to the Grand Canyon,” said Mom the next morning.

Abbi stretched, begged for five more minutes of sleep, and rolled over under the covers. Finally, she leapt out of bed and gobbled up her breakfast, remembering that today she would see her cousin Addie.

As they were leaving the hotel, Abbi stopped and barked, “Wait! I need to mail my thank you card for my bandana to Mrs. Ruth and the postcard I bought at Mount Rushmore for my pen pals in Miss Paling’s class.” Abbi rushed back inside and politely asked the concierge to mail the note and postcard. Then, it was time to hit the road.

"Are we there yet?" whined Abbi.

"Not quite, Ab. It's over 1,000 miles from Mount Rushmore to the Grand Canyon and we've only been driving 30 minutes."

Abbi paced the backseat and decided a nap would help pass the time. When she woke up, they were in Colorado, where they would spend the night with Addie, a chocolate Labrador.

Addie and Abbi chased each other around the garden, both excited to be reunited.

"Did you find my bandana at the Colorado Rockies stadium? Was it on the field? The dugout? Or in the stands? Come on, Addie, did you find it?" barked Abbi.

"Sorry, Ab. I looked all over the ballpark but I struck out. It wasn't there," barked Addie.

"Oh no! I just knew you would find it. You, Kutta, and Pretzel are the only friends I haven't heard from."

Abbi pouted on her cousin's favorite blanket for a long time but finally decided it would be way more fun to hike in the mountains and play with Addie. Exploring outdoors always made her feel better.

Tomorrow, Pretzel and Kutta would call with news from the beaches of Florida and California.

In the morning, Abbi and Rachael said goodbye to their Colorado family. They had a long day of driving ahead of them to make it to the Grand Canyon by nightfall.

"Arizona, here we come!" howled Abbi with her head out the window, her fur blowing in the wind.

Hours later they heard a "Bzzzzz! Bzzzzz! Bzzzzz!"

"Mom, your phone is ringing! It must be Kutta!"

Reagan the Jeep pulled off the road so Rachael could take the call.

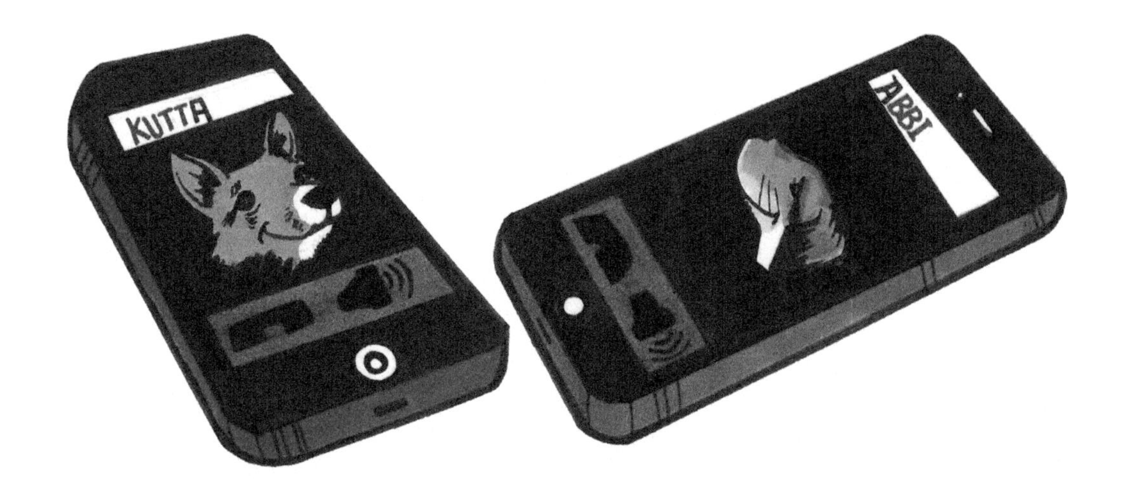

“Hi, Kutta! Abbi has been anxiously waiting for your call.”

Abbi barked at the phone. Kutta replied with a big bark.

“Sorry it took me so long to call you back, Abs. It took my short Corgi legs longer than I expected to look up and down the beaches of San Diego. Did you know there are sea lions there? Those things are gigantic!” barked Kutta.

“Yeah! They smell but they’re really neat to see. Did you find my bandana? The stars and stripes would stand out in the sand,” barked Abbi.

Kutta hesitated. “Um, uhh, I didn’t find it. Sorry. I know this bandana is important to you with the parade and all.”

“Oh, it’s okay, Kutta. Thanks for trying. You’re a great pal,” barked Abbi. “I’m bummed you and Pretzel didn’t find my bandana, but I’ve had a great time seeing some of my favorite landmarks in America again and making new friends. And I love that all my friends are having adventures, too. Pretzel said he saw a dolphin off the coast of Florida, and you got to see sea lions. America is filled with treasures.”

“You bet it is!” barked Kutta. “I had a blast! Travel safe, Abbi, and good luck on the bandana hunt.”

Miles and miles later after several pit stops for gas and sweet tea, they made it to the majestic southern rim of the Grand Canyon. Abbi and Rachael hopped out of Reagan and headed to Mather Point, where they had spent most of their visit earlier that year.

"Woah! I forgot how vast the Grand Canyon is," Abbi exclaimed. "Remember when we were here the park ranger said the park covers over one million acres?"

"Yes! She said some of the rocks can be dated back over 2,000 million years," said her mom.

They gazed into the canyon for a long time. Then they walked to the visitor center to check the lost and found and buy a postcard.

"Bzzzzz! Bzzzzz! Bzzzzz!"

Rachael answered her phone. "Howdy! Yes, this is Rachael. It is great to hear from you, Ranger Dan." She put the phone on speaker for Abbi.

"Hello? Ranger Dan?" barked Abbi.

“Hi, Abbi! I have great news! You know how your friend Einstein posted flyers of your missing bandana all over New York City? Well, they worked. I just got a call from the National Park Service. A junior park ranger found your bandana at the Statue of Liberty!”

“Really?” Abbi spun around in circles and let out a big howl.

“I can’t believe it! Mom! They found my bandana. It was hanging out with Lady Liberty this whole time! We’ve got to drive to New York right now!”

“Wait!” shouted Ranger Dan through the phone. “Your bandana is already in the mail to your home in Texas. It will be waiting for you.”

A celebration was in order. That night, Abbi and Rachael enjoyed their favorite treat, ice cream, at the Grand Canyon under a blanket of stars.

Abbi couldn't wait to share the good news with Miss Paling's class and all her friends.

The next morning, Abbi waved goodbye to the Grand Canyon. The bandana was on its way home to Texas, and so were they. It was time to prepare for the parade, which was just a week away.

"Mom, I was thinking about the parade, and I have a favor to ask," barked Abbi.

"Sure, Ab, what is the favor?"

"Since my friends helped look for my bandana, would you ask Mayor Stewart if they can all be in the parade with me? You know, as a thank you for being great friends and helpers?"

"That is a wonderful idea."

The lights were bright in Tucumcari, New Mexico.

Everyone was happy to stop for the night, especially Reagan.

The search to find the missing bandana had taken them over 5,000 miles! After dinner at a roadside diner, they walked along historic Route 66, looking at old motor hotels and quirky shops. Just one more sleep and they would be back in the Lone Star State.

The next day, Abbi and her mom yelled "Welcome to Texas!" as Reagan drove them over the state line. It was a long drive across their home state, so they filled the hours by singing along to their road trip playlist.

"We've got so much to do when we get home. I need to take a bath and get my nails trimmed so I look my best waving from the float. We have to decorate the float, wash my bandana, and get ready for my friends to come to town for the parade. It was so great of Mayor Stewart to allow them to be in the parade with me."

“We will get it all done, I promise,” said Rachael. “I bet our friends in Miss Paling’s class and our family will help decorate the float. Abbi, look where we are!”

Abbi leapt up and put her front paws on Reagan’s console to get a better look.

“Home!”

She sprang out of the Jeep and galloped to their mailbox. Finally, her signature, one-of-a-kind, patriotic bandana was safe and snug around her neck.

“I am never losing this again!” she woofed.

Abbi and her friends and family spent the next week getting the float ready.

While her mom, Aunt Jodi, and grandparents put on the finishing touches, Abbi went to bed with her beloved bandana tucked safely under her pillow.

The next morning, she woke with excitement. Parade day had arrived! Mayor Stewart greeted Abbi and her mom at the parade site. Reagan the Jeep was proudly pulling Abbi's America-themed float—red, white, and blue bunting flapping in the wind—ready for his parade debut as well.

"Abbi, my furry friend, are you ready to lead the parade? You've got your signature bandana on I see!" said the mayor.

"Yes, sir, I'm ready! Thankfully my friends helped me find my bandana just in time. I'm excited to share this big day with them and all my family!"

Abbi's grandparents, aunts, uncles, cousins, and friends were all there to walk in the parade with her. They cheered as the mayor announced to the whole town that Abbi was this year's grand marshal!

Abbi and her canine friends were on the float ready to get the parade started. Rachael checked Abbi's bandana one last time to make sure it was tied on tight.

The high school band began to march in front of Reagan, playing patriotic tunes, and just like that the parade was moving. The streets along the parade route were filled with people. Abbi and her friends waved and tossed candy.

When Abbi heard the students from Miss Paling's class cheer from the side of Main Street, she let out a big bark and beamed from ear to fluffy ear with her tail swooshing side to side.

Her American adventures had led her to the front of her hometown parade.

Abbi couldn't be more proud to be the grand marshal and share her love of America with everyone.

Independence Hall, Philadelphia, PA
Did you know: The Liberty Bell, weighing over 2,000 pounds, rang in Independence Hall. It is now on display for visitors to see. The bell bears the inscription "Proclaim Liberty Throughout All the Land Unto All the Inhabitants thereof" and has become a symbol of freedom around the world.

United States Capitol, Washington, D.C.
The United States Capitol building is home to the legislative branch of our government, the U.S. Congress, made up of the U.S. House of Representatives and the U.S. Senate.

Mount Rushmore National Memorial
Did you know that President Washington's face on the monument is 60 feet tall and that the memorial took 14 years to complete?

Great Smoky Mountains National Park
The Great Smoky Mountains National Park is home to a variety of wildlife, including the American Black Bear, chipmunks, wild turkeys and a variety of fish, birds, and reptiles.

Washington Monument
The Washington Monument in Washington, D.C., honors our nation's first president, George Washington.

Colorado Rockies Game
Abbi enjoyed her first MLB game, America's favorite pastime, at the Colorado Rockies game in Denver, Colorado.

CPSIA information can be obtained
at www.ICGtesting.com
Printed in the USA
LVOW05*0348250117
522039LV00007BA/13/P